The Purse

Kathy Caple

Houghton Mifflin Company

Boston

To my niece, Molly Ann Caple

Copyright © 1986 by Kathy Caple

Printed in Japan

DNP   10   9   8   7   6   5   4   3   2

Library of Congress Cataloging-in-Publication Data

Caple, Kathy.
  The purse.

  After spending her money on a purse, Katie is now
faced with the problem of getting some money to put
into it.
  [1. Handbags—Fiction. 2. Money—Fiction] I. Title.
PZ7.Cl7368Pu   1986   [E]   86-2889
RNF ISBN 0-395-41852-6
PA   ISBN 0-395-62981-0

Clinkity clinkity clinkity clinkity.

Katie shook the Band-Aid box up and down
as she marched into the living room.

"Why must you make so much noise?" said
her sister Marcia. "What's in that box anyway?"

"All of my money," said Katie. She poured
the money out of the box. "I have two dollars
and thirty cents. I'm rich."

"Keeping money in a Band-Aid box is for babies,"
said Marcia. "Why don't you buy yourself a purse?"

"I never thought of that," said Katie.

"You really should get one," said Marcia.
"If you want, you can come to the store with me
and I'll help you pick one out."

"All right," said Katie. She put the money
back in the box and gave it another loud shake.

When they got to the store Marcia showed
Katie the purse department.

"Do you see anything you like?" asked Marcia.

"Oh, yes," said Katie, "I like that one.
How much is it?"

"It's two dollars and thirty cents," said Marcia.

"I have just enough money," said Katie.

"I'll buy it."

She went to the cash register and paid for it.

"I guess I won't be needing this
anymore," said Katie.
She tossed the Band-Aid
box into the trash.

Katie and Marcia started home.
Katie took out her new
purse and looked at it.
It was so clean and bright.
"It even smells good,"
said Katie.

Then she shook it.
"It doesn't make a noise," said Katie.
"That's because it's empty," said Marcia.
"I don't have any more money," said Katie.
"You can put other things
in it," said Marcia.

As soon as Katie got home, she went up
to her room. She put a crayon and a pencil
sharpener in her purse. She put a mirror and
two red buttons in it. Then she added a pink
eraser and two small seashells.

She gave it a shake.
Thump thump thump.

Katie poured everything
out of the purse.

11

Then she went to Marcia's room.

"I wish I had my money back," she said.

"Well," said Marcia, "maybe you could earn some money doing extra jobs around the house."

Katie thought for a minute.

"I know. I could clean your room
and I'll only charge twenty-five cents."

"It's a deal," said Marcia.

First Katie hung up all of Marcia's clothes.

Then she picked up all the records.

She stacked the books back on the shelves,

she swept the floor,

and last of all she made the bed.

Marcia gave Katie two dimes and a nickel.

Katie put the coins in her purse.
She gave it a shake.
Plunk plunk plunk.
"I need more money," said Katie.

She went downstairs.

"Papa, do you have any jobs I can do?
I need some money to put in my new purse."

"Let's see now," said Papa, "You could finish
clipping coupons out of these magazines.
I'll pay you sixty cents."

Katie picked up a magazine and turned the
pages. There were lots of coupons to clip.

She clipped soap coupons and cereal coupons.
Coupons for sponges, catfood, and milk.
There were coupons for peanut butter and pudding.

The pile grew bigger and bigger.

Finally she was finished.

"You were a big help," said Papa. "Here's
your sixty cents and an extra quarter to go with it."

"Wow! Thanks," said Katie.

Then she took out all of
her money and counted it.
She had one dollar
and ten cents.

She put the money back in her purse and
gave it a shake.

Plunkity plunkity plunkity.

Katie could hardly wait to earn more money.
She went outside.

"Mama, do you have any jobs I can do?
I only charge sixty cents an hour."

"That's a real bargain," said Mama.
"You can help me in the garden."

"All right," said Katie.

First they pulled some weeds.

Then Mama showed Katie
how to use a hoe.

Then they planted new seeds.

After that, Katie
watered everything.

When they were finished, Mama
gave Katie one dollar
and twenty cents.

Katie took the money out
of her purse and counted it.
She had two dollars and thirty
cents, the same as she had before.
She put the money
back in the purse.
It was getting heavy.
Then she shook it.

Clunkity clunkity clunkity.
Katie went into the house.

Papa was getting ready to go grocery shopping.

"Can I go with you?" asked Katie.

"There's something I want to buy."

"Sure," said Papa.

When they got to the store, Katie looked
up and down the aisles.

Finally she found what she wanted. She picked out a new box of Band-Aids and went to the cash register to pay for it.

"That'll be two dollars and thirty cents," said the sales clerk.

Katie gave all of her money to the clerk. Then she waited for Papa to finish buying groceries.

Katie and Papa started home.

Katie took out the new
box of Band-Aids
and looked at it.
Papa looked too.

Then Katie looked at the purse.
"I'm all out of money again,"
she said.

"I have an idea," said Papa.
"I could buy your Band-Aids for two
dollars and thirty cents, and you can
keep the box."
"Oh, yes," said Katie.

She took all of the Band-Aids out of the box
and gave them to Papa.

He gave her the money.

Katie put the money
in the Band-Aid box
and put the Band-Aid box
inside her purse.

She gave it a shake.
Clinkity clinkity clinkity clinkity.
Katie smiled.
She shook her purse the rest
of the way home.